This edition is published by Armadillo,
an imprint of Anness Publishing Ltd, Blaby Road,
Wigston, Leicestershire LE18 4SE; info@anness.com

www.annesspublishing.com

If you like the images in this book and would like to investigate using
them for publishing, promotions or advertising, please visit our website
www.practicalpictures.com for more information.

© Anness Publishing Ltd 2013

A CIP catalogue record for this book is available from the British Library.

Publisher: Joanna Lorenz
Project Editors: Belinda Wilkinson and Richard McGinlay
Editorial Consultant: Jackie Fortey
Production Controller: Wendy Lawson

PUBLISHER'S NOTE
The author and publishers have made every effort to ensure that this book
is safe for its intended use, and cannot accept any legal responsibility
or liability for any harm or injury arising from misuse.

Manufacturer: Anness Publishing Ltd,
Blaby Road, Wigston, Leicestershire LE18 4SE, England
For Product Tracking go to: www.annesspublishing.com/tracking
Batch: 1012-22469-1127

A Storyteller Book

Beauty and the Beast

Retold by Lesley Young

Illustrated by Annabel Spenceley

ARMADILLO

There was once a very rich merchant, who lived in a huge, grand house with his three daughters. They were all very pretty, but the youngest daughter was the prettiest. She was always smiling, showing two dimples in her creamy skin, and her smile was so lovely she became known as Beauty.

Her sisters sprawled about all day on silk couches, admiring themselves in mirrors, but Beauty had better things to do. She spent a lot of time visiting the old, poor people in the cottages nearby, and cheering them up.

Lots of young men wanted to marry the sisters. The two oldest always refused because they were waiting for a duke or a prince. However, Beauty always thanked the young men, but said she was too young to marry.

"Also," she explained with a smile, "I want to stay at home and look after Father when he's old."

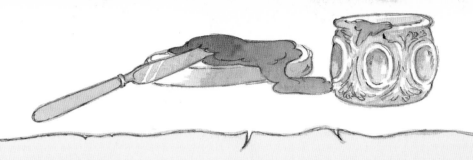

One day at breakfast, a servant brought in a letter on a silver tray. The girls' father read it and went as white as the tablecloth.

"All my ships have been lost in a storm at sea. We are as poor as church mice now, so we must move to a small cottage and find what work we can."

"Work?" snapped the oldest sister in horror, while the middle sister piled even more strawberry jam on her bread, in case she couldn't have any more for a while.

"Don't worry, Father," said Beauty, going around to him and patting his forehead, "we'll be all right as long as we're all together."

"Let's go to a ball tonight. Perhaps we can find a couple of rich men to marry us," said Beauty's sisters.

But now that they were poor, no one wanted to marry them.

"Where is Beauty? We would marry her tomorrow, because she would be sure to make us happy," all the young men said.

The sisters were furious to hear this, and scowled so much that they looked quite cross and ugly.

After a short time the merchant and his daughters had to move out of their grand house. They all went to live in a tiny cottage in the heart of the countryside. When they moved in, it was damp and unwelcoming. The two elder sisters hated their new home, and did nothing but complain bitterly.

"How can we be expected to live in a place like this?" they moaned, huddling together beside a smoking fire.

Beauty, however, tied on an apron and set to work. She painted the rooms and put flowers everywhere. She smiled so kindly at the woodcutter who lived down the lane, that he left bundles of wood for her. Soon she had good fires going in all the rooms, and the cottage was filled with the smell of baking bread. While she worked, she sang, and she still managed to find things to make her happy.

Her sisters lay in bed all morning and then sat around
complaining, while Beauty was up with the birds to welcome
her father downstairs with a cheery,

"Fried mushrooms for breakfast! I found a real treasure trove
of them in the wood."

"You are my treasure now, Beauty," he would say, with tears
in his sad old eyes.

They lived like this for a year. Then, one day, a messenger rode to the cottage and told the merchant that one of his ships had turned up. It had not been wrecked, after all, but had taken shelter in a far-off country, and had now finally arrived back at the port, filled with goods.

"I must go down to the coast and sort things out," said the merchant. "Now, what will I bring you back?"

"New dresses – at last!" said the elder sisters. "And face cream, and silk stockings, and precious gems, and perfume, and hats with feathers on them and . . ."

"What about you, Beauty?" asked her father. "You haven't asked for anything yet."

"I would like a rose," said Beauty at once. "A beautiful pink rose."

The merchant was away for a long time, but at last he set out for home, loaded down with presents for his daughters. He had found everything on their list except for a rose, and it was now winter so nothing was growing except thorn bushes.

The merchant was not far from home, when suddenly a great snowstorm blew up and swirled round him. The snow was so thick that his horse could hardly see where it was going.

The merchant rode along, the snow settling thickly on his hat. He hoped he would soon find a house where he could seek shelter. In the distance he could hear hungry wolves howling, which made him anxious, and he urged his horse on.

At last, just when he thought he could go no farther, the merchant saw a light shining dimly through the snowflakes and he rode toward it. He was amazed to find that the light was pouring out of the windows of a splendid palace.

The merchant knocked on the door, but no one answered. His horse was tired out, so he put it in the empty stables, where he found fresh water and oats waiting. Then the merchant trudged back through the deep snow to the palace, and pushed the heavy door which creaked slowly open.

"Hello?" called the merchant, but there was no answer, so he walked through the hall into a large room with a roaring fire. There was a wonderful smell of roast chicken, and he saw a table, set for one with gold plates and knives and forks.

The merchant took off his wet coat and hat and wandered over to the table, where a large roast chicken glistened in the firelight.

"I'm sure that whoever lives here won't mind if I sit down," he thought.

So he sat at the table and waited. And waited.

When the gold clock on the wall struck eleven, the merchant could stand it no longer. He grabbed the roast chicken, which was still hot and moist, and tore it into pieces and began eating. He had never tasted anything as good. There were plates of roast potatoes, crispy onion rings, and peas that tasted as if they were just out of the garden, even though it was winter.

When he had washed all the food down with some good red wine, the merchant noticed a silver bowl of strawberries and cream on the table.

"I could have sworn that wasn't there a moment ago," he said to himself, before he ate them. The strawberries were the reddest and ripest he had ever eaten, and tasted delicious.

By now the merchant was feeling very sleepy. He set out to explore the palace, making his way through many grand rooms. At last he came to a room with a fire glowing in the fireplace and a canopy bed with the covers turned down. Without thinking, the merchant took off his clothes and slipped between the sheets, which were crisply laundered and smelled of lavender. At once he was fast asleep.

"Cock-a-doodle-do!"
    The merchant woke with a start and sat up in bed. The sun was streaming into the room, and he jumped up and looked out of the window.

He rubbed his eyes. Was he still asleep and dreaming?

The merchant looked down on a garden that was in full, summer bloom. All the snow had vanished, and instead there were huge beds of roses, and grass as green as emeralds.

His old, travel-stained clothes had gone, and there was a new suit of clothes laid out in front of the fire. He washed with a jug of hot water that was steaming in front of a mirror, and dressed in the new clothes, which fitted him perfectly.

Back in the dining hall, the foods he liked best were heaped in silver dishes: juicy sausages, fluffy scrambled eggs, muffins that melted in his mouth and a pot of hot chocolate.

He ate his fill, and stood up to leave.

"Whoever you are, thank you!" he shouted before he went off to saddle up his horse.

The merchant was leading his horse out through the beautiful garden, when he remembered his promise to bring back a rose for Beauty.

"The garden is full of roses," he said to himself, "and the owner of the house has been so generous, he will not miss just one."

So the merchant stopped and picked the largest, pinkest rose he could see.

At once there was a huge roar, and a beast appeared in front of him. It was so horrible to look at that the merchant almost fainted.

"So this is the thanks I get!" roared the beast, "I give you shelter from the storm, I feed you and lay out new clothes, and what do you do?"

The merchant trembled.

"You steal the things I love most – my roses. Well, for that you will die."

"I . . . I only wanted one rose as a present for the thing I love most – my daughter, Beauty," stammered the merchant. "Is there nothing I can do to save my life?"

"Nothing," roared the beast, "unless, that is, you promise to return, bringing with you the first thing that greets you when you get home."

When he heard that, the merchant smiled with relief. He had a little black dog that was always first to run out to meet him when he came home after a long journey.

So he agreed, put the rose carefully in his hat, and quickly set off home.

Beauty was shaking a quilt out of a bedroom window in the cottage, when she saw her father riding in the distance, with the rose in his hat bobbing up and down.

"I don't believe it – he's found a pink rose!" she cried, and she rushed out of the cottage and ran down to the front door to meet him. The little black dog, meanwhile, was dozing in front of the fire.

"My dear daughter," said her father to Beauty. "I have paid a dreadful price for this rose." And he told her how he had promised to send the beast the first thing that met him.

"Don't worry, Father," said Beauty, "I will gladly go. The beast can't be as bad as you say, and perhaps he will let me come home if I ask him kindly."

The next day, Beauty and her father were both red-eyed and tired, because neither of them had slept a wink.

"It's no good, you have to keep your promise," said Beauty, "But I'm sure it will work out for the best."

"Yes – off you go," said her sisters, who were busy trying on the fine dresses their father had brought home for them.

So Beauty and her father galloped off through the bare and chilly countryside. Both their horses seemed to know the way to the beast's castle, as if they had been there many times.

As soon as Beauty and her father rode into the palace grounds, they were surrounded by summer blooms and lush rose bushes.

"It's magic!" said Beauty, her eyes shining. "All these roses – in the middle of winter.

I can hardly believe it."

They tied up their horses and went inside the palace. In the dining hall, there were now two places set, and a delicious meal was waiting for them under silver covers.

"Come, Father," said Beauty bravely, "I will eat if you will."

They were just finishing large, ripe peaches that tasted of honey, when there was a terrifying roar outside the door, which grew louder and louder.

Beauty dropped her peach and stared at the door, which opened
very slowly. There stood the beast – looking even more horrific
than her father had described. He had put on his best clothes of
a red velvet cloak and a white lace collar, but these only made
him look even more ugly.

He sat down beside them at the table and said, "So this is the
Beauty for whom you plucked my rose?"

"It is," said the merchant sadly, "she ran to meet me when
I went home, but has insisted on coming back with me."

"I am glad that you did," said the beast to Beauty, and she
was surprised to hear that his voice was soft and gentle.

"You must leave in the morning," said the beast to Beauty's
father. "Rest assured your daughter will be quite safe with me."

The next day, Beauty's father left her and rode sadly home.
Beauty spent the day walking in the grounds among the sweet
smelling roses.

After dinner, she was sitting in her room when there was a
knock at the door.

"May I come in?" asked the beast.

"Of course," said Beauty, pulling another chair up to the fire.

The beast spoke so kindly to her, that when she looked into
the flames, she quite forgot how ugly he was.

The next night, he came to her room again.

"Help yourself to the peaches and grapes that grow in my
garden," he said, and his voice was kinder than ever.

On the third night, the beast brought Beauty a large bunch of pink roses.

"Oh, how lovely!" she gasped.

"Will you marry me?" asked the beast, sinking to his knees.

"I can't, my dear beast," replied Beauty.

"Then I will surely die," said the beast.

Two large tears rolled down the beast's ugly face, and he left the room.

Beauty soon discovered that the mirror in her room was magic. Sometimes she saw herself when she looked in it, and sometimes she saw a picture of other people and things that were happening somewhere else.

One day, she looked in the magic mirror and saw her poor father lying on his bed, looking very ill. She also saw her sisters in another room. They were happily curling each other's hair and laughing. They seemed to have quite forgotten their poor sick father.

When the beast came to her room that night, Beauty was very sad and told him what she had seen.

"I must go home and look after him," she said. "If I don't, he will surely die."

"And what about me?" asked the beast. But when Beauty began to cry, he agreed to let her go home for a week, as long as she promised to come back to him when the time was up.

The beast gave Beauty a special pink rose and said, "Hold this rose and wish, and it will take you wherever you choose. It will also bring you back to me, so don't forget your promise."

He left her, with a swish of his cloak, and Beauty at once wished herself back in her father's cottage.

She was just in time. Her father was very ill, but as soon as he saw Beauty he felt better. She made him a soup with special herbs that she had brought from the beast's garden, and he felt his strength come flooding back.

"Who does she think she is?" said her sisters crossly. "Fresh herbs at this time of year indeed, while we have to make do with old turnips!"

The sisters grew very jealous when Beauty described the beast's palace, with its wonderful rose garden and gold plates.

"I suppose our wooden bowls are not good enough for you now?" they jeered.

When the week was almost up, the sisters hatched a plan.

"Why should we have to slave away here, while she wanders about in her magic garden eating grapes? We'll stop her leaving, and then we'll see if her precious beast comes to get her," said one of the sisters.

"Oh, how exciting!" said the other.

So the two sisters pretended to be very fond of Beauty, and showered her with hugs and kisses.

"If you leave now, we're sure Father will become ill again," they said, and they went into the kitchen and sniffed onions to make themselves cry.

"We can't bear to think of you going back to that beast," they howled.

Beauty was so soft-hearted and kind that she agreed to stay for another week.

"Then I really must go back," she said, "because I promised."

She was rather surprised to find just how much she missed the beast, and their talks every evening by the fire.

At the end of the second week, Beauty kissed her father and told him not to worry.

"I am not frightened of the beast now," she said. "I know he would never do me any harm."

Her sisters were bored with waiting for the beast to come roaring up to the cottage, and didn't try to make Beauty stay any longer.

Beauty held the pink rose in her hand and wished herself back in her room in the beast's palace.

It was evening, and she waited for the beast to come, as usual, to talk to her, but he never came.

Beauty spent a sleepless night, tossing and turning, and in the morning she set out to look for the beast.

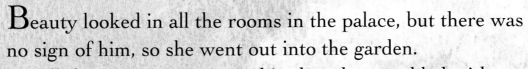

Beauty looked in all the rooms in the palace, but there was no sign of him, so she went out into the garden.

All the roses were covered in dew that sparkled with rainbows as she walked in her bare feet on the cool grass.

"Dear beast, where are you?" called Beauty.

At the very edge of the garden, where the grass changed into the winter countryside, Beauty saw the beast, lying on the ground.

"He is dead," she thought. "I broke my promise and I have killed him."

She knelt down, took his rough hairy hand, with its long claws, in her hands, and began to cry.

When her tears fell on his face, the beast opened his eyes and looked up at her.

"You forgot your promise to me, Beauty, and now I must die," he sighed.

"No," cried Beauty through her sobs, "What can I do to save you."

"Will you marry me?" asked the beast for the second time.

"I will," replied Beauty at once.

There was a bright flash of light, the beast vanished, and in front of Beauty stood a handsome prince.

"Where is my beast?" she asked, looking round.

"Here he is," laughed the prince, holding out his arms.

"A wicked witch put a spell on me, turning me into a beast until a beautiful girl agreed to marry me. You saw beneath my ugly disguise, and you have saved me."

The prince sent a gold carriage to fetch Beauty's father and sisters for the wedding.

So Beauty and her gentle prince were married, and, for the first time in years, the palace was filled with flowers and laughter.

After the wedding feast, Beauty's two sisters could be seen, scurrying around the garden bending over and carefully examining each rose bush.

"What on earth are they doing?" asked the prince.

"I think they are looking for a magic rose to wish for their own prince," said Beauty smiling, "but magic like this could surely only happen once in a lifetime."